I Want to Ride the Tap Tap

Danielle Joseph
Pictures by Olivier Ganthier

FARRAR STRAUS GIROUX
NEW YORK

To Delle, Marley, Makhi, and Naya—with all my love.
And to Haiti—mwen adore w. —D.J.

To my art family—Mica, JDG, and Didier. To my mentors,
to every Haitian child in the world, and to Savannah D.
Haiti forever, bel enspirasyon! One love. —O.G.

Farrar Straus Giroux Books for Young Readers
An imprint of Macmillan Publishing Group, LLC
120 Broadway, New York, NY 10271

Text copyright © 2020 by Danielle Joseph
Pictures copyright © 2020 by Olivier Ganthier
All rights reserved
Color separations by Bright Arts (H.K.) Ltd.
Printed in China by RR Donnelley Asia Printing Solutions Ltd., Dongguan City, Guangdong Province
Designed by Gene Vosough
First edition, 2020
1 3 5 7 9 10 8 6 4 2
mackids.com
Library of Congress Control Number: 2020910179
ISBN 978-0-374-31214-5

Our books may be purchased in bulk for promotional, educational, or business use. Please contact your local bookseller or the Macmillan Corporate
and Premium Sales Department at (800) 221-7945 ext. 5442 or by email at MacmillanSpecialMarkets@macmillan.com.

On Lendi morning, Claude and Manman walked Papa to the tap tap stop.

"Where are you going?" Claude asked a lady holding a basket.

"To the market to sell my mangoes."

"Bon bagay!" Claude said. "Can I go to the market, Manman?"

"No, Claude," Manman said. "You have to go to school."

Claude waved goodbye to Papa. He dreamed of mangoes.

On Madi, the tap tap rolled down the mountain.

"Where are you going?" Claude asked the man carrying a bucket and a pole.

"Fishing," the man replied.

"Bon bagay!" Claude asked Manman, "Can I catch some fish?"

"No, Claude. It's a school day."

Claude imagined reeling in a jumbo fish for Manman's gumbo.

On Mèkredi, Claude played with marbles while they waited for the tap tap.

"Where are you going?" Claude asked a woman balancing a tub of straw on her head.

"To make hats."

"Bon bagay!" Claude pleaded, "Can I go, too?"
Manman sighed.
"Not today," Papa said.
Claude wished he could weave a hat for
Manman to shade her from the sun.

On Jedi, Claude spotted a man with a box of paints
and a paintbrush waiting for the tap tap.
"Where are you going?" Claude asked.
"To paint a picture of the beach."

TAP TAP

"Bon bagay!" Claude jumped up and down.
He looked at Manman. "I know, not today."
Claude wanted to paint a picture
of his very own tap tap.

On Vandredi, a man banged on a steel drum. *Ping, pling, ping, pling.*

"Where are you going?" Claude asked.

"To perform with my band," the man said.

"Bon bagay!" Claude hummed to the music.

"Can I go see him play? Please?!"

"Not today," Manman said.

PLING

PING

PING

PING

PING

PING

TAP
TAP

Claude stomped to the beat of the drum. He was missing all the fun.

On Samdi, Claude woke
up early. He felt sad.
No tap tap.
No mangoes.
No fishing.
No weaving.
No painting.
No drumming.

Only chores at home.

On Dimanch morning, after church, Papa said, "Let's go to the tap tap stop."

"Why?" Claude looked up at Papa. He saw
a twinkle in Papa's eye.

The tap tap clanked to a halt.
"Welcome aboard," the driver said.
Claude dashed inside.

When the tap tap turned left, Claude slid right.
When the tap tap turned right, Claude slid left.

As the tap tap bounced up and
down the street, Claude asked,
"Papa, where are we going?"
"You'll see," Papa said.

Finally, the tap tap stopped. Papa stood up. "We're here."

Claude hurried off the tap tap and ran to the beachfront.
"Bon bagay! Look who's here!" Claude shouted.

The mango lady
gave Claude a mango.
"Mèsi," he said.

The fisherman called to Claude, "Hey, help me reel in this fish."

Claude grabbed the pole and tugged hard.

"Would you like to make a hat?" the hat lady asked.
"Yes, for my mother," Claude replied.

The lady showed him how to weave the straw. Over and under, over and under.

The artist asked Claude, "Would you like to paint?"
"Yes!" Claude beamed. "My very own tap tap."
"Well, then, let's get started, tipiti."

At the end of the day, Claude picked up his
feet and danced to the beat of the drum.

He clapped as the band played his favorite songs.

Before Claude knew it, all his friends from the tap tap stop were swaying and sashaying.
Papa took Manman's hand and spun her around.

PING

PING PANG

PING

Haitian Creole Glossary

Bon bagay! (*bon ba-gai*): This is good stuff!

Manman (*man-man*): Mama

Mèsi (*meh-see*): Thank you

Ou la la (*ooo la la*): A phrase to express surprise
    or excitement, like "Wow!" or "Yay!"

Tipiti (*tee-pee-tee*): Little one

Lendi (*len-dee*): Monday

Madi (*mah-dee*): Tuesday

Mèkredi (*meh-kre-dee*): Wednesday

Jedi (*je-dee*): Thursday

Vandredi (*van-dre-dee*): Friday

Samdi (*sam-dee*): Saturday

Dimanch (*dee-mar sh*): Sunday

Tap tap (*tap tap*): A colorfully decorated, privately owned vehicle that can be as large as a school bus or as small as a pickup truck. No two tap taps are the same! The name comes from the passengers tapping their fingers against the sides of the bus to signal to the driver that they want to get off.